P9-AGT-810

I'm Going To READ!™

These levels are meant only as guides;
you and your child can best choose a book that's right.

UP TO 50 WORDS

Level 1: Kindergarten–Grade 1 . . . Ages 4–6

- word bank to highlight new words
- consistent placement of text to promote readability
- easy words and phrases
- simple sentences build to make simple stories
- art and design help new readers decode text

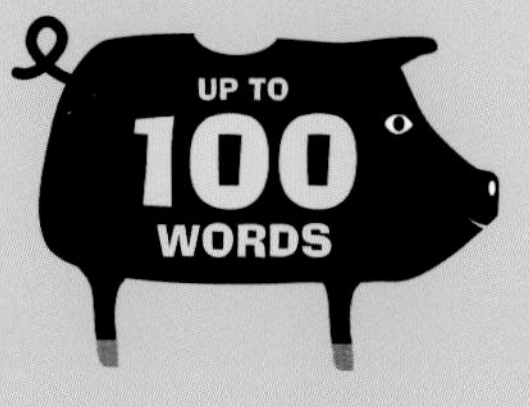

Level 2: Grade 1 . . . Ages 6–7

- word bank to highlight new words
- rhyming texts introduced
- more difficult words, but vocabulary is still limited
- longer sentences and longer stories
- designed for easy readability

Level 3: Grade 2 . . . Ages 7–8

- richer vocabulary of up to 200 different words
- varied sentence structure
- high-interest stories with longer plots
- designed to promote independent reading

MORE THAN 300 WORDS

Level 4: Grades 3 and up . . . Ages 8 and up

- richer vocabulary of more than 300 different words
- short chapters, multiple stories, or poems
- more complex plots for the newly independent reader
- emphasis on reading for meaning

LEVEL 4

Library of Congress Cataloging-in-Publication Data Available

2 4 6 8 10 9 7 5 3 1

Published by Sterling Publishing Co., Inc.
387 Park Avenue South, New York, NY 10016
Text © 2007 by Harriet Ziefert Inc.
Illustrations © 2007 by Lon Levin
Distributed in Canada by Sterling Publishing
c/o Canadian Manda Group, 165 Dufferin Street,
Toronto, Ontario, Canada M6K 3H6
Distributed in the United Kingdom by GMC Distribution Services,
Castle Place, 166 High Street, Lewes, East Sussex, England BN7 1XU
Distributed in Australia by Capricorn Link (Australia) Pty. Ltd.
P.O. Box 704, Windsor, NSW 2756, Australia

I'm Going To Read is a trademark of Sterling Publishing Co., Inc.

Printed in China
All rights reserved

Sterling ISBN-13: 978-1-4027-3084-9
ISBN-10: 1-4027-3084-5

For information about custom editions, special sales, premium and
corporate purchases, please contact Sterling Special Sales
Department at 800-805-5489 or specialsales@sterlingpub.com.

Small Potatoes Club

Pictures by Lon Levin

Sterling Publishing Co., Inc.
New York

CHAPTER ONE

The Gang

Hi. We're a group.

I'll introduce you to everybody.

There's Roger, Sam, Chris,

Molly, Maria, Carlos, and Spot.

Roger wears glasses.

Sam has freckles.

Chris is tall, and Molly is not.

Maria has braids, and Carlos does not.

And Spot is Spot. (He's also Molly's dog.)

Sometimes we play ball.

We play until everyone starts arguing.

Then we have to think of something else to do.

Sometimes we have races.

When Molly is last,

Maria shouts, “Hurry up!”

And Molly answers, “But I’m running as fast as I can!”

Sometimes we play follow-the-leader.

Maria likes to be the leader.

Sam does not.

“Follow me and do what I do!” shouts Maria.

“That’s what you always say,” complains Sam. “You’re too bossy!”

One day someone had a really great idea.

"Let's start a club and build a clubhouse."

Sam thought it was his idea.

But Molly said it was hers.

Sam and Molly argued until someone said,

"Stop arguing and let's get started."

Maria said, "We need rope and string—

some sheets and blankets too!"

"Is that all we need?" asked Chris.

"No," said Sam. "We'll also need branches

to make a roof."

"I know where to find two big branches,"

said Carlos. "Who will help me carry them?"

"I will," said Molly.

Arf! Arf! barked Spot.

"I'll go ask my mother for some rope,"

said Roger.

“Me too,” said Chris. “We’ll need a lot of rope.”

“And we’ll ask for sheets and blankets,” said Maria and Sam.

“Hurry everybody! Be back here with the stuff in twenty minutes,” yelled Molly.

CHAPTER TWO

Building a Clubhouse

"Let's get going," said Molly.

"We have to tie a rope between the trees."

Molly stood near one tree.

Sam stood near another.

"This is not easy," said Sam.

"Nothing's easy," said Chris, "but we can do it!"

Three more ropes had to be tied around trees. Carlos and Roger helped with the tying. When they were pulled tight, the ropes formed a square.

"Now we're ready to hang the blankets," said Chris. "If we use two blankets in the front, we'll have a door."

"Spot, get out of the way," said Molly. "If you don't move, you'll be stepped on."

“Get the roof branches,” yelled Molly.
“And watch what you’re doing!”

Molly, Sam, and Roger put the
roof branches in place.

“Boy, what a neat roof,” said Sam.
“It lets the light in.”

“And the rain too!” grumbled Roger.

The clubhouse was finished.

It looked pretty good.

"All we need is a sign," said Maria.

"What shall we write on it?" asked Sam.

“Silly question,” said Maria. “We should write the name of our club!”

“Well, what’s the name?” asked Carlos. Everybody started to think. But no one spoke up.

Finally Roger said, “I think I have a really good idea. We should call our club the Small Potatoes. Does anybody know the potato rhyme?”

“Do you mean, ‘One potato, two potato, three potato, four . . . ’?” asked Maria.

"That's what I mean," said Roger. "Everybody takes a turn at being a potato. I'll start. I'm one potato!"

"Two potato!" said Sam.

"Three potato," said Chris.

"Four potato," said Molly.

"Five potato," said Maria.

"Six potato," said Carlos.

Arf! Arf! said Spot.

“We’re seven potatoes, including Spot,”
said Roger.

“Seven potatoes—that’s our small gang,”
Molly shouted.

“Are any more potatoes allowed?”
asked Chris.

“No more potatoes,” said Roger, “at least
not for now!”

CHAPTER THREE

The Gang Votes

Here we are.

Today we're having a meeting.

"Let's vote," said Chris.

"Yes's stand up and no's stay down," said Molly.

Chris looked around and counted. "There are four yes's and two no's—plus one arf-arf!"

"But what did we vote for?" asked Maria.

No one knew the answer to Maria's question.

Then someone said, "Let's vote about whether or not we should play soccer. Yes's stand up and no's stay down."

Again Chris looked around
and counted.
"There are five yes's and one no
plus one bow-wow!"

"So let's play," said Sam.

“I want to be the captain of one team,” said Maria.

“You’re too bossy,” said Chris.

Maria answered, “If you want, you can be the captain of the other team, but I called it first!”

“Let’s stop arguing and start playing,” said Carlos.

So we divided up into teams.

The game started.

Sam kicked from the center.

Roger got the ball and began dribbling

toward the other team's goal.

“Kick the ball—kick it hard to me!”

shouted Molly, who loved to win.

Roger tried to pass to Molly,

but Carlos stole the ball.

Carlos tried to kick to Maria,

but the ball went out-of-bounds.

Roger got a free throw.

Then Molly scored a goal.

The ball was back in the center.
Sam kicked—and guess who
got the ball?

"Get out of the way, Spot!"
yelled Carlos.

"Stupid dog!" shouted Sam.

But all the shouting didn't
help one bit.
Spot had the ball and he
wouldn't let it go.
Spot sat in the middle of the field.
He smiled. He looked very happy.

17

We all looked at him and couldn't help smiling back.
Someone said, "It's all right, Spot. We still love you!"

Molly patted Spot on the head.

Then Chris said, "I guess our soccer game is over for today. Let's do something else."

CHAPTER FOUR

For Members Only

There was a meeting the next day.

Carlos banged two rocks together and said, "Will this meeting please come to order!"

When everyone was quiet, Carlos asked, "Is there any old business?"

Maria answered, "I have some old business."

"Here is the model of the tyrannosaurus
that I made," she continued. "Does anybody
want to hear how I made it?"

"I think your model's nice," said Roger,
"but I don't really want to hear
how you made it."

"I agree," said Molly. "I'd rather do something."

"I know what we can do," said Chris.
"Spot, come here. I need you."
Spot came.
Chris asked everyone to hide their eyes.
"Don't look!" Chris said.
Chris and Spot worked together.
Nobody knew what they were doing.
Every now and then Chris would say,
"It'll just be a few more minutes."

"Hurry up!" said Maria. "We're tired of waiting."

"Okay," said Chris. "Now you can open your eyes."

What do you think we saw?

There was Spot, looking just like a Tyrannosaurus rex!

Everybody started to laugh.

"You don't scare us!" shouted Carlos.

Then Carlos asked, “Is there any new business?”

“I have an idea. Let’s make membership cards,” answered Sam.

“Cards are easy to make. All you need are markers and scissors—and some stiff paper,” said Roger.

“I like Sam’s idea,” said Maria.
“A membership card shows you belong.”

“Let’s get started,” said Sam.

While she was working on her card, Molly asked, "Does anyone think other kids should be allowed to join the Small Potatoes?"

"I don't," said Roger.

"We're a small club," said Carlos, "and we should stay small."

"A big club would be better, but we can't fit more kids in this clubhouse," grumbled Roger.

"Well, we could have members who have their own clubhouses," said Carlos.

Chris asked, "How can we do that?"

Carlos answered, "We can give out Small Potatoes membership cards. They can build their own clubhouses and have their own meetings."

"Gee, you're smart," said Maria. "We get
members, but our small clubhouse
doesn't get crowded!"

"Let's vote about taking in new members," Roger said.

Somebody asked for a secret ballot.

After Roger had counted all the slips of paper, he said, "Everybody voted 'yes.' So other kids are welcome to join the Small Potatoes." (You can too!)

"Great," said Maria.

Molly said, "I move to adjourn this meeting."

"I second the motion," said Sam.

"Okay," said Roger. "Before we go, everyone should know they're invited to the next meeting of the Small Potatoes Club.
And don't forget to make membership cards!"

"See you at the next meeting!"

Small Potatoes FUN

Build a clubhouse with some friends.

When you're all done, have a meeting.

Since you are now a member of the Small Potatoes Club, make a membership card for yourself. You can copy the one below or invent your own.

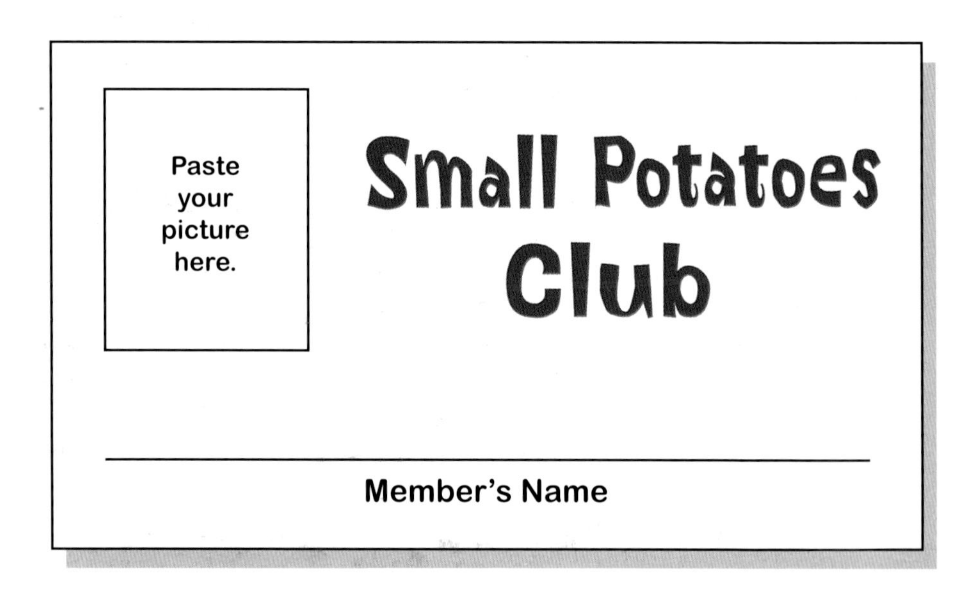